# TRIPLE THE TOMFOOLERY!

Written by The Grand Writer

Illustrated by Cabolt - X

Dear Reader,

Thank you for choosing this comic, I hope you enjoy reading it just as much as I enjoyed working on it or even more!

I'm Cabolt-X, a freelance 2d artist and animator with an avid interest in comics and cartoons. Drawing has always been something I enjoyed doing since childhood. I have always dreamed of drawing comics and creating animations. I started my freelancing journey in 2020 during the lockdown, this has given me the opportunity to work with several amazing clients, including Grand Writer, who have given me the avenue to gradually make my dreams a reality.

I would never have made it this far without help, so I want to specially thank my parents, especially my late Mum; she was the biggest supporter of my dream, my siblings, Ifeanyi and Oluomachi, who motivate me a lot and my friends especially Victor and Loveth, who have supported me on this journey. I would also love to thank "Talented Hands" for rekindling my passion for drawing in 2016 when I was beginning to lose interest and my buddies, Collins and Kinato, who ushered me into digital drawing, taught me a lot I know about it and have been a huge source of inspiration in my career. This is the first comedy comic and the first 4-koma comic I have worked on, and it's all thanks to Grand Writer, who gave me this amazing opportunity, I really appreciate your time and patience with me. I had a great deal of fun working on this with you! I would also like to thank you, the reader, again for purchasing this comic, your support is highly appreciated.

Cabolt-X

*Cabolt-X*

Thank You Readers of the Grandest Tales,

I, the Grand Writer, want you to thank you grandly for the purchase of this book. A single comic of many to come. I want to thank God, my Pastor, and her family. My family and friends. My readers and fan. I thank those who have been in my life, and those that will in the future. I thank the very existence of good will and happiness in the world.

I thank all those that will read this book and find something funny, inspiring, possibly even life-changing. I know this is a silly comic book, yet it was written by a silly *grand writer*. So again, thank you.

Since 2020, Grand Verse Comics have been creating grand tales. Here to more years of grand stories. As well, more years of such wonderful readers.

Sincerely Thanking You,

The Grand Writer

*The Grand Writer*

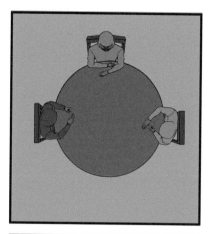

The "3 Grand Writers" have gotten along greatly together. Almost like brothers in a sense.

Surprisingly, the doppelgänger effect never came into play.

The Grand Writer must have such a positive personality. Or a loving nature.

Or possibly, the Grand Writer hold their negative emotions tightly locked up. It would explain a lot.

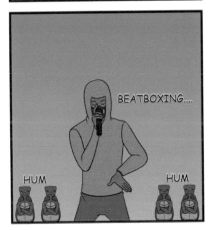

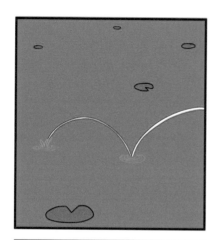

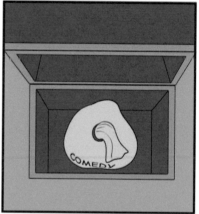

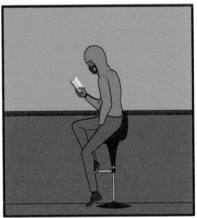

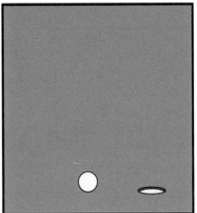

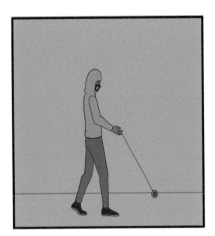

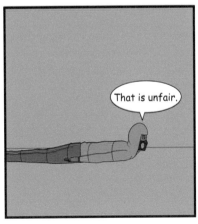

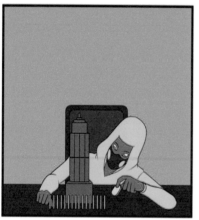

# Creator's Page

The Grand Writer, a mysterious writer who loves to tell grand stories. Sometimes silly, sometimes strange, sometimes even serious. Yet, overall Grand!

Cabolt-X, an inspiring artist and embolden gentleman. Given either a pen, pencil, marker or paint, nothing is too far to draw! Tag him in as an extra hand, to create bold new art!

Made in the USA
Columbia, SC
07 July 2024

38238428R00022